MERRY [CHRISTMAS] 1995

TO [...]

LOVE,

LEE, JON, AMOS

THE
LUTE'S TUNE
GINA FRESCHET

Illustrated by Steve Cieslawski

Doubleday

New York   London   Toronto   Sydney   Auckland

A DOUBLEDAY BOOK

PUBLISHED BY DELACORTE PRESS
Bantam Doubleday Dell Publishing Group, Inc.
666 Fifth Avenue, New York, New York 10103
DOUBLEDAY
and the portrayal of an anchor with a dolphin
are trademarks of Bantam Doubleday Dell Publishing Group, Inc.

Library of Congress Cataloging-in-Publication Data:
Freschet, Gina.
The lute's tune / Gina Freschet ; illustrated by Steve Cieslawski.—1st ed.
p. cm.
Summary: Kaal, a young orphan boy, is summoned by the king, who
hopes that the music from his lute will revive his dying daughter, Arianne.
[1. Lute—Fiction. 2. Death—Fiction.] I. Cieslawski, Steve,
ill. II. Title.
PZ7.F889685Lu   1992
[Fic]—dc20   90-14084   CIP   AC
ISBN 0-385-41167-7

RL:2.9
Text copyright © 1992 by Gina Freschet
Illustrations copyright © 1992 by Steve Cieslawski

Printed in Hong Kong
March 1992
1 3 5 7 9 10 8 6 4 2

To my mother, Berniece,
whose loving support
has guided me.
—G.F.

IT was a time of hardship in the land, a time of struggle and labor. The poor were sad and tired from their chores.

In the province of Elsmere lived a peasant boy named Kaal. He was an orphan and very poor. He had barely enough money to buy a loaf of bread. But one thing he did have, and this he treasured above all things. He had a lute, a lute made of cherry wood with golden strings and a neck of polished cedar. It had been handed down through the ages by his family and given to him by his mother when she died.

Kaal sat in the orchards from morning to night, playing his lute beneath the trees. He could make it sing with the voice of many waters. He could make it soft and sweet like the murmur of a mother to her child, or deep and rich like the songs of the men working in the fields. And at night, when the moon went down, he could make it lull the villagers to sleep.

People came from far and wide to listen to the songs. Women brought their children when they were sick or fretful and the tones of the lute would comfort them. When Kaal played in the fields the music made the day seem shorter. The farmers' hearts became light and their work was made easy. Old Jubal, the lame peddler, claimed that the tunes soothed his crooked bones. The widow Mitza forgot her sorrow in the silvery notes. And Leah, the silent girl, listened to the lute's sweet song and forgot the shame of her pockmarked face.

Bᴜᴛ some said Kaal was mad to play for the people all day. They said to him, "Fool. Why don't you sell the lute and buy yourself bread to eat?" But Kaal replied, "The music I play is more filling to me than the bread I could buy with a fortune."

So he continued to play the lute through the spring, bringing blossoms to the trees. He played into summer, making the crops grow full and ripe. And finally autumn came. It was time for the harvest, a time to feast and to dance and give thanks for a good season.

Each autumn Kaal played at the harvest festival. The village girls put on red skirts and danced the circle dance. The men linked arms and laughed while their wives prepared foods and sang at the ovens. Everyone was joyful. The lute sang merrily, calling the people to dance. When darkness fell, great fires were lit so the feasting could continue.

On the second night of the festival, a stranger appeared in their midst. He was dressed in the dark robes of royalty, a servant to the King. The people were afraid when they saw him, for the King was a stern and powerful man. But the servant passed among them silently, going directly to Kaal, who sat playing the lute near the fire.

THE music stopped. Kaal saw that the man's face was troubled. "What need have you, brother?" he asked.

The stranger said, "I am Zepha, the King's minister."

"I am Kaal."

"My master's house is troubled," said Zepha. "The King's daughter, Arianne, is ill. She can neither eat nor drink but sleeps all day and night."

"I am sorry," said Kaal. "Is there nothing to help her?"

Zepha bent his head. "The King has discharged us throughout the land to search for cures and medicines, but none have worked."

Kaal absently brushed the strings of the lute and sent a chord into the air. "You can help," Zepha told him.

"I? How can I help?"

"Your music . . . I have never heard such sweet tones. When you played I was filled with warmth and my heart was lifted. Perhaps you could help the princess with your songs."

"I would, gladly," Kaal replied. "But what have I to do in the palace of the King? I haven't even sandals for my feet."

"That is no matter," said Zepha eagerly. "I will take you to the King. He will welcome anyone who can help his daughter."

B UT the villagers cried, "Don't go! We need the lute's tune for a fruitful harvest." Kaal smiled at them, saying, "Friends, don't worry. I will return." Then he told the King's minister, "Lead on. I must go where the songs are most needed." He wrapped his ragged cloak about him and went with Zepha into the night.

B Y morning they had left Kaal's homeland far behind. The palace of the King stood in the distance, a mighty structure of marble and crystal. Its towers rose to the sky, challenging the mountain peaks. By midday they had arrived. The surrounding gardens were rich with fruit trees, exotic flowers and birds of every shape and hue. As they approached Kaal said, "I can never enter such magnificence."

"Outside it is beautiful," said Zepha. "But inside there is sickness and sorrow. Our King grows thin with worry and the girl never stirs."

They mounted the front steps and entered the inner court. The atrium was crowded with doctors, alchemists, magicians and holy men, stroking their beards and muttering.

"ONLY balsam and coltsfoot will work," croaked one.

"No, no," said another. "A poultice of arrowroot applied to her eyes will awaken her."

"You're an old quack," sneered a magician. "We must draw a circle around her bed and fill it with steaming stones. Then I will chant over her for seven hours and she will surely be cured."

"You are all wrong," said Zepha. The men turned to stare at him and the ragged boy who followed. "Your cures have all failed," continued the King's minister. "Each day our King becomes more distracted and the maiden's sleep becomes deeper. Only this boy might rouse her."

"What?" they snorted. "That wretched little swineherd?" And they all began to laugh. "No doubt the stench of his clothes might rouse her," said one.

"Or perhaps in a fretful moment she might catch a glimpse of him and laugh herself awake," scoffed another. Zepha turned to Kaal. "Ignore them. Wait here while I seek an audience with the King."

KAAL sat at the base of a pillar. He looked at the splendor surrounding him, at the high domed ceiling and the thick tapestries that hung from the walls. The old men resumed their quarrels. None of them looked at Kaal.

He felt alone and uneasy, so Kaal lifted the lute and began to play. The tune came forth lightly, but with a touch of sadness in its voice. Then it began to build, gaining strength and courage. The song rose fuller until it resounded in the great dome of the ceiling. It seemed to push open the palace doors and a cool breeze blew into the room. When Kaal stopped playing there was silence. The old men stared at him, speechless. "Never have I heard such sweetness," whispered one.

"It is enough to coax the angels from their thrones," said another.

"Boy, where did you learn such a song?" asked the magician.

"It is not my song," replied Kaal. "The lute plays itself." They were all amazed. The tune still echoed in their ears. Their mouths hung open. Some even wept.

Zepha returned and motioned to Kaal. "Come with me. The King will see you. That is, if he can. He is like one in a trance these days. A dark hand holds his heart."

They mounted a wide staircase and passed down a hallway. The lute hung from Kaal's shoulder strap. Its smooth cedar neck brushed his side. The boy touched its strings and said softly, "See what a fine place you have brought us to."

A T the end of a long hall stood a door that reached to the ceiling. Zepha swung it open and ushered Kaal inside. Then the great door closed behind him and the boy was alone in a vast indoor garden.

The glass walls seemed to rise to the sky and the ceiling was hidden by trees. Mimosas with their feathery blooms swayed above and young willows brushed the floor. Their branches were filled with parrots, canaries and mist-colored larks. Cranes and pheasants strutted proudly across the paths.

Kaal walked through the garden slowly, filling his nostrils with the scent of the flowers. Then, between the trees, he saw a man. The man was sitting on a stone bench with his head in his hands and a long gray beard trickled into his lap. He seemed unable to hear the calls of the birds or to smell the perfume of the blooms. He looked sad and pained. Kaal went to his side but the King did not see him. He stared straight ahead as if blind. Kaal sat down at his feet. He took the lute, cradled it in his lap for a moment, and then began to play.

KAAL touched the strings. They hummed. It was the sound of a mother hushing her child. The tune was simple, slow and gentle. It brushed the tips of the ferns and the birds fell silent, ashamed of their own songs. Then, slowly, the King began to stir. The whispers of the lute blew through his beard and he began to sit up. Straighter and straighter he sat until, finally, with his hands planted firmly on his knees and his head lifted, he regained the full stature of his royalty. The tones of the lute grew quieter, softer, and then with a final hush, were stilled.

The King blinked his eyes. He looked around. Then he saw Kaal sitting on the floor with the lute.

"Who are you, boy?"

"I am Kaal. I was sent to play for you."

"I thought it was my own dear mother singing," said the King. Kaal smiled. "Shall I play more?"

"No," the King said gently. "Not now. I'm afraid my heart would break if you did." He put a hand on Kaal's shoulder. "How can one so young play with the breath of heaven?"

"I don't know," said Kaal. "I just play. It is like a wind rushing through me until I am borne away and only the song remains."

"Just so," the King murmured. "It is the same for the listener." The King stood up. He stretched and said, "This is a lovely garden, is it not?"

"As lovely as the forests of my home," said Kaal.

"You are a strange boy. Your song has made me new. Come, you must play for my daughter. If any can raise her it is you."

THE King led Kaal through a doorway hidden by rosebushes. They climbed a narrow staircase. Up and up it arched and curved. Finally, they reached the top and stood before a small door. The King stooped to enter and Kaal followed him into a dimly lit chamber. There stood a bed veiled with mesh.

On the bed lay a young girl. She was clothed in rose and her skin was as pale as her gown. She did not move. Kaal approached and looked at her. She was lovely. Her dark hair spilled out over the pillow and her eyelids were barely lavender. But there was no blush to her cheeks, no color in her lips. Her breath was very faint.

The King took her lifeless hand and kissed it. His tears fell upon her wrist. "Arianne, my daughter, awake," he entreated. But she did not stir.

The King turned away. "You stay with her," he told Kaal. "Play for her. I cannot bear to see her this way." Then he replaced her frail hand and slowly left the room.

KAAL continued to gaze at the sleeping face, so white and still. Then he went to the window and sat on the ledge overlooking the garden. It was twilight. He could see the full moon rising above the mountains. He held the lute close to his breast. Then he shut his eyes and began to play.

He plucked a single string. The note hung in the air, somber and lonesome. Then another joined it, and another. The tones were low and throbbing, the sounds of mourning. The tune called out to Arianne, beseeching her to wake. But she did not move. The tune grew stronger, rising from deep within the lute's belly. The song reached into the cavern of death to reclaim Arianne. It ran through her hair and touched her brow. Kaal watched her closely. There was a flicker of her eyelashes. Her lips parted slightly. Kaal's heart tightened. He plucked the strings of the lute firmly, strengthening the call.

Then he sent a high note soaring into the air. It was a note higher than any he had ever struck. It pierced the room like a falcon's cry. It melted into its own echo.

But it was not enough. Arianne's lips closed. Her eyes were motionless beneath their lids and she lay as before. The high note dissolved and then disappeared. Kaal bent his head. He was exhausted. The lute had not awakened her. Kaal sank to the floor. The lute slipped from his fingers and he fell asleep.

FROM the dark side of her slumber, Arianne heard something. She heard a song, a song more exquisite than that of a hundred nightingales. She did not know where it came from, she only heard it calling her. The notes rose and rippled and entered her heart. Her blood quickened. She felt like a running stream, faster and faster until, finally, a single note sprang upward and with it went Arianne's soul. Her spirit leapt from her body and she floated to the ceiling of her room.

She looked down and watched herself sleeping. She felt like a breath of air. Then she saw Kaal asleep near her bed with the lute beside him. "Surely," she thought, "this boy is a magical shepherd, for he has struck a chord to the other world."

Arianne descended like a bird and hovered near Kaal's head. She reached down and ruffled his hair. But in his sleep Kaal's hand accidentally brushed the lute. A single string sounded. Arianne shivered. She felt the sound pulling her, drawing her back to her sleeping self. She could not resist. Her spirit returned to her bed and re-entered her slumbering body.

KAAL awoke suddenly. The curtains of Arianne's bed moved like ghosts. Kaal sat up, remembering his dream. He had dreamt that Arianne woke up. She had floated down to him like a cloud and had touched his hair. Kaal quickly went to her bedside. But she lay undisturbed. There was no crease in her pillow, no sign that she had stirred. Kaal stayed with her until the dawn was near. A blue mist arose from the hills. Kaal was saddened. He felt he had failed.

WHEN the King heard that the lute had not awakened his daughter, he was downcast but still hopeful. "That's all right, my son," he told Kaal. "Play for her again tonight, and the next, and for as long as it takes to rouse her. You shall be a guest in my court."

So Kaal stayed at the palace. He was given a fine tunic to wear and he wandered through the halls. He went below to the large kitchens and watched the cooks at their ovens. They offered him food, but Kaal was not hungry. He visited with the gardeners. Zepha showed him the great library and the music room. Kaal marveled at the harps and spinets and instruments there. Zepha told him that many fine composers and musicians had entertained the court. "But," he added, "none could rival the songs of your lute."

All day the strings of the lute murmured at Kaal's side, impatient to play. But he waited.

WHEN darkness fell and all the palace was asleep, Kaal slipped into the moonlit garden beneath Arianne's window. He thought that if he played outside beneath the moon and stars they would lend strength and magic to his song.

He sat down and gazed up to the girl's window. Kaal ran his hand down the smooth neck of the lute, whispering, "We must wake her tonight. You must sing like the waters of life."

TONIGHT the tune was different. Kaal was hopeful and his heart was uplifted. The lute did not call Arianne with the voice of sorrow, but coaxed her like a running river, inviting her to taste its waters. The music trilled and each note laughed with a silvery tongue.

Arianne heard its call. She heard it dimly through her heavy sleep. The tune ran on, flooding the garden with its voice. Then Kaal struck the magical note. It flew up to the sky like a ringing bell and Arianne's spirit sprang up to capture it. She opened her eyes. She had risen to the ceiling of her room, free of her body's sickness. She tingled all over. She drifted out the window, not bothering to look back at her sleeping self.

SHE floated as lightly as a thistledown. She saw Kaal below her. He seemed to have a hundred fingers, they strummed so quickly over the strings of the lute. Arianne looked around her. The trees had arms and all their leaves quivered like tiny fish. The stars overhead moved in a timeless march. Everything pulsed with its own heartbeat. "Surely," thought Arianne, "this is the other side of the world, where all things are stripped of their shadows."

Light with wonder, she wanted to fly beyond the garden walls like an eaglet over the land. But she wanted Kaal to come with her. Together they would fly away on the lute's tune. Arianne drifted down near Kaal's head. This time he saw her, fluttering like a white shadow in the air. He saw the trees through her gown and her hair streamed out like a silvery web. For an instant he thought he was dreaming, but Arianne whispered to him, "Come with me. Leave your body as I have done and we will go together."

"Arianne," gasped Kaal. "Are you alive?"

"Yes," she answered. "More alive than ever before. Your song has shown me the other side of the world. It is radiant here. Come."

But Kaal was disturbed. "Arianne," he said, "you must return to your body. Your father grieves. You must return."

"No," she said. "The body is sick and filled with pain. It cannot fly. It cannot see the wonders which I see now. If my father knew the beauty of this place, he would gladly let me stay. Your music has freed me."

"Then the music shall capture you again," said Kaal. He began to play the lute.

"No," she pleaded. *"Don't play the note that sends me back."*

BUT Kaal kept playing. He plucked the golden strings until they rang. Arianne shuddered. Something pulled at her. She was drawn back to her bedroom window. With a last little cry, she flew into her room and once again entered her sleeping form.

Kaal laid down the lute. He was afraid and confused. Arianne's soul was happy, but he had sent her back to her body. Her mournful cry still hurt his ears. He felt he had made a terrible mistake. He thought of the King, how he grieved for his daughter. But if the other world was as lovely as Arianne said, surely her father would let her remain there. Kaal stroked the lute and looked at the strings in wonder. "You are the key to another land. It must be very beautiful there."

KAAL did not sleep that night. He sat in the garden and thought of the other world. Arianne's words came back to him. "I am more alive than ever before." Kaal wanted to see this other world. He wanted to leave his body and fly with Arianne between the palace spires. The lute's tune had freed her, but why not him?

It was because Kaal's body was stronger and held tight to his spirit. But Arianne had been sick for many days and her body was weak. That was why she had left it so easily.

Kaal thought all night. When the moon sank low and the sun rose to take its place, he was tired. But still he did not sleep. He sat with the lute on his knees. It seemed both wondrous and forbidden to him. Its strings glistened in the morning light.

THE King was uneasy. He lay in bed listening to the morning lark. He thought about his dream. It disturbed him greatly. Last night he had dreamt that Arianne had risen. She had left her body and floated into his room like a puff of smoke. She had whispered in his ear, "Father, do not grieve. I am alive in a world you cannot see."

The King had reached for her and cried out, "My daughter, do not leave me!" But his hand passed through her own as if through water.

Arianne tried to comfort him. "I have not left you. Only my body sleeps. It is like a cage which I have fled."

But the King wanted his daughter as she was before. He wanted to watch her gather flowers from the gardens and dance.

"Arianne," he begged her. "Return to me." But she said simply, "I have never left." Then he awoke.

THE day was long for Kaal. He had not been able to eat or sleep since leaving his home. He sat in the garden all afternoon, thinking of Arianne and the other world. Finally, the sun went down. The birds ceased their calls and the moon rode upward on the sky. As he waited for the night to deepen, Kaal felt lightheaded. When at last the palace was dark, he went to the bench below Arianne's room. He looked up to her window. He felt dizzy and strange. He took a deep breath, bent his head over the lute and began to play.

It was an eerie tune, high and thin. It piped like a lonely shepherd's song, an ancient song from far away. The notes were at first slow and halting, but each was clear and true. As he played, Kaal watched Arianne's window. Then he shut his eyes and plucked the magical note. The piercing sound flew upward and carried Kaal with it. His spirit shivered from his weakened body and was released.

Kaal floated upward, trembling. He felt light; he wanted to laugh. Below, his body slept, bent over the lute. Kaal opened his arms. He wanted to embrace the night. The stones on the ground were glittering jewels. The birches were made of glass; their leaves were like diamonds. Each object was brilliant and bright, as if a dark veil had been lifted from the world.

KAAL looked up and saw Arianne drift out of her window. He flew up to greet her. She laughed and put her fingers in his hair. "You see," she said merrily, "how splendid it is?"

They touched hands, rolling over and over on the breeze. They dipped low to the ground and Kaal said, "Look! I have no shadow."

"Of course not," laughed Arianne. "You have no body to cast one with."

Kaal shouted with joy. "It is more glorious than anything I could ever imagine."

"Everything is alive here," said Arianne. "The true hearts of all things are exposed."

Together they flew above the garden and chased each other between the trees. Then they rolled over onto their backs and floated along, gazing up at the stars.

"I have never seen so many," Kaal murmured.

"No one can see what we see now," replied Arianne.

"Here we will live together, forever young and never to die."

It seemed to Kaal that he knew the names of all things and the place of each person who lived on the earth. The knowledge so filled him that he thought he would burst. He looked out over the land, which stretched below like a flowering cloak. Then he felt a sudden pain. He remembered his homeland. He thought of his people, how they toiled all day. How could he remain in this perfect world while they were so burdened with care?

ARIANNE circled high above him. The moonlight sparkled in her hair and her laughter was like chimes. "Come, let's race," she called to him. But Kaal thought of Old Jubal, the lame peddler, and of the widow Mitza, and Leah, the silent girl. Their only happiness was in listening to the lute's tune. He had promised them he would return. Could he abandon them now?

A light flickered on in the palace. The King was up and out of bed. He was taking his candle to Arianne's room. He felt he must see his daughter, to try and speak with her, even if she could not hear him. He hurried down the halls and opened her door. The room was cold. He went to Arianne's bedside and took her hand. It was icy. He looked about for Kaal. Then he went to the window and saw the boy's body asleep in the garden. But there was something else. There were two shreds of mist hovering above the trees. They looked like wisps of smoke. The King clutched his heart, remembering his dream. He recognized the spirit of his daughter. He rushed from the room and ran down to the garden.

KAAL drew Arianne to him. "I cannot stay," he told her. "I must return to my people. They need me."

"No. Do not leave me." For an instant she was afraid.

"Arianne, please listen . . ." But she would not. She flew away from him.

The King burst through the hedges. "Arianne!" he cried. "Come back!" In panic, he ran to Kaal's sleeping form. "What have you done to her? You have bewitched my daughter with your music!"

But Kaal's body slept on. The lute slipped to the ground. The King picked it up and swung it over his head.

Kaal's spirit swooped down. "No!" he shouted. "You must play the note which brings us back."

The King's beard blew in the wind like a madman's. His face was stricken but he heard and heeded Kaal's words. He began plucking the lute as if crazed. He pulled the strings with all his might. *He will break it,* thought Kaal. *The lute will not play for him.*

Kaal knew he must return to his body. But could he? He summoned all his strength. He shut his eyes and hung suspended in the air. Kaal willed himself to go back, repeating over and over, "I must return. I must return. Return . . . return . . . return . . ." His spirit grew weaker and weaker. It began to fade.

Arianne called to him, "Come back!" But her voice was distant to his ears. His soul shivered like a puff of frost growing smaller and smaller . . . and then, with a whisper, it vanished.

KAAL re-entered his body. He sprang to his feet. "Stop!" he shouted. "You're pulling too hard!"

But the King jerked the strings like an archer. He plucked harder, faster, and then . . . it snapped. The string that played the magical note snapped with a pang that broke the night.

The King raised his head and let out a howl. "Arianne! Do not leave me!" He slumped and wept over the broken string. It coiled like a thread of light. "I have lost her forever," he moaned.

But Arianne's spirit sailed down to him. "Father, Father, do not weep," she told him. "I am always with you. You shall hear my voice in the wind and feel my touch in the rain. I shall visit you in dreams." Then she kissed her father's cheek and turned to Kaal.

"Dear minstrel," she said, smiling. "I would have flown with you between the earth and sky. But I know you must return. Go, bring to your people the song of the other world. Let them hear it and have hope."

"Someday," said Kaal, "I shall join you."

"Yes," she whispered. "And I will be waiting."

Then she touched his brow with her fingertips and, lifted on the wind, she disappeared.

THE garden was silent except for the sound of weeping. The King sat on the bench with his head in his hands. Kaal went to him and quietly took up the lute. There was one string less, but the boy cradled the instrument. And then he began to play.

The tune began gently, as a dove ruffles its feathers. The notes were soft and fragile. Their clear tones beat against the King's breast and swept away his tears. Then the tune took flight, fanning upward into the sky.

The King raised his eyes, following the path of the song. His heart rose with it and he was filled with peace. Never had he heard so tender a sound. Never was the garden so enchanting. The trees were crowned with stars. He knew now that his daughter was happy. He knew that Arianne was soaring in a world of light, which he could only glimpse. And he knew that someday he, too, would see that world.

The King bent his head and was quiet.

K AAL walked across the fields. His steps were light and the lute swung gently at his side. Soon he would be home. He touched the medallion at his breast, a token of friendship and farewell from the King. There was a chill in the air. Winter was coming. Kaal was returning in time to warm the hearts and lift the spirits of his people. He saw the first hut of his village and heard a joyful cry. The children had seen him and were running from their homes, shouting, "Kaal is back! He's returned!"

All the people gathered to hear of Kaal's journey. Mitza was there and Old Jubal, who grinned and croaked, "At last, my pain shall be eased." Silent Leah stood at the edge of the crowd, hiding her scarred face and watching Kaal through her fingers. The people looked at him anxiously.

But Kaal did not speak. He only smiled and touched the cheek of one of the children. "If I can," he said to himself, "I will show this child, and all who follow, that there is reason to hope and be joyful. That their spirits will not be broken by the cold of the night or an empty bowl. I will bring them to know of another world."

Then he lifted the lute and began to play.